Dear Parents and Educators,

Welcome to Penguin Young Readers! As parents and educators, you know that each child develops at their own pace—in terms of speech, critical thinking, and, of course, reading. Penguin Young Readers recognizes this fact. As a result, each Penguin Young Readers book is assigned a traditional easy-to-read level (1–4) as well as a Guided Reading Level (A–P). Both of these systems will help you choose the right book for your child. Please refer to the back of each book for specific leveling information. Penguin Young Readers features esteemed authors and illustrators, stories about favorite characters, fascinating nonfiction, and more!

Mo Jackson: Run, Mo, Run!

LEVEL 3

GUIDED READING LEVEL **J**

This book is perfect for a **Transitional Reader** who:
- can read multisyllable and compound words;
- can read words with prefixes and suffixes;
- is able to identify story elements (beginning, middle, end, plot, setting, characters, problem, solution); and
- can understand different points of view.

Here are some **activities** you can do during and after reading this book:
- Creative writing: Pretend you are Mo. Write a journal entry about your day at school and the track meet. What was your favorite part of the day?
- Reading with expression: Although many transitional readers can read text accurately, they may read slowly or not smoothly, and pay little or no attention to punctuation. One way to improve this is to read out loud with the child. For example, read pages 18 to 19 in this story out loud. Ask the child to pay special attention to how your voice changes when you come to different punctuation such as commas, periods, or exclamation points. Then have the child read another page out loud to you.

Remember, sharing the love of reading with a child is the best gift you can give!

This book has been officially leveled by using the F&P Text Level Gradient™ leveling system.*

*Penguin Young Readers are leveled by independent reviewers applying the standards developed by Irene Fountas and Gay Su Pinnell in *Matching Books to Readers: Using Leveled Books in Guided Reading*, Heinemann, 1999.

For Deborah, my amazing daughter-in-law,
who somehow gets everything done. —D.A.A.

For Joe Ron Bellman, who taught me the
importance of the Pythagorean theorem—
and of brutal interval workouts. —S.R.

Penguin Young Readers
An imprint of Penguin Random House LLC
New York

First published in the United States of America by Penguin Young Readers,
an imprint of Penguin Random House LLC, 2020

Text copyright © 2020 by David Adler
Illustrations copyright © 2020 by Sam Ricks

Visit us online at penguinrandomhouse.com

LIBRARY OF CONGRESS CATALOGING-IN-PUBLICATION DATA IS AVAILABLE
ISBN 9781984836823

Manufactured in China

1 3 5 7 9 10 8 6 4 2

RUN, MO, RUN!

by David A. Adler
illustrated by Sam Ricks

Penguin Young Readers
An Imprint of Penguin Random House LLC

Mo Jackson is in a hurry.

He eats his lunch.

He puts a cherry jelly donut

in his pocket for later.

"Finish eating,"

he tells his friend Jenna.

"We need to get ready."

There is a track meet after school.

Mo, Jenna, and Dov are in Class 2B.

They will be in the relay race

against students from

Class 2M.

Dov will run first.

He will pass the baton to Jenna.

START

FINISH

Then Jenna will give

the baton to Mo.

Mo will finish the race.

"I'm done with lunch," Jenna says.

"Let's get ready."

The straw from her milk

is their practice baton.

"You wait ahead," Jenna tells Mo.

"I'll run to you and pass the baton.

Then you run to the finish line."

Mo waits for Jenna.

When she gets close,

Mo starts to run.

Jenna can't pass the baton.

"No! No! No!" Jenna tells him.

"Don't go so early."

They try again.

Jenna passes the baton
but Mo drops it.

"No! No! No!" Jenna tells him.

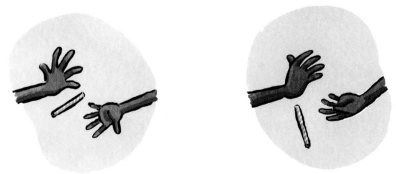

Ring! Ring!

"We have to go to class," Mo says.

Jenna tells Mo, "And you

have to hold on to the baton."

Mo takes the baton to class.

"Throw out that dirty straw,"

Mo's friend Fran tells him.

"It's not a straw.

It's a baton."

Mo's class is learning

to read AT words.

Mo's teacher says,

"CAT and BAT are AT words.

So are SAT and MAT."

Under his desk,
Mo passes the straw
from one hand
to the other.

"Mo," his teacher says.
"You need to listen."

Ring! Ring!

Mo's teacher tells the class,

"Get ready for the track meet."

The other team wins the

50-yard dash.

Mo's team wins the

softball throw.

Next is the long jump.

Mo gets close to watch.

His friend Fran wins it.

She jumps so far

that she crashes into Mo.

"Look!" Jenna tells Mo.

"Your pocket is red!

You are a jelly mess."

Fran crashed into

Mo's jelly donut pocket.

Mo reaches into his pocket.

He takes some donut and eats it.

"Yummy," he says.

"Dov, Jenna, and Mo,"
their teacher calls.

"It's time for the relay race."
Mo hurries and
gets in place.

Dov and Barry start the race.

Dov is fast.

Barry is faster.

Barry passes the baton to Amir.

Dov passes the baton to Jenna.

Jenna is fast.

Amir is faster.

Dov, Jenna, and Mo

are losing the race.

Amir tries to pass the baton
to Lula.

Lula drops it!

She stops to pick it up.

Jenna puts the baton

in Mo's hand.

Mo doesn't drop it.

He can't.

It is stuck in jelly.

"Go, Mo!" his friends call out.

"Go, Mo, go!"

his mom and dad call out.

They came to watch.

Mo runs past Lula.

She picks up her baton.

She runs.

She tries to catch up to Mo.

"Go, Mo, go!"

his mom and dad cheer.

Mo runs fast.

He crosses the finish line.

He runs into his parents' arms.

Dov, Jenna, and Mo

won the relay race.

Mo's team won

the most races.

"Good job.

For winning," his teacher says,

"we'll have a special treat

tomorrow at snack."

Jenna says, "I hope it's ice cream."

"I hope it's jelly donuts,"

Mo says.

"Yummy!"